There's a Mouse in the House!

For Josh and Leah,
with love from Grandma.
—W.C.L.

Library of Congress Cataloging-in-Publication Data is available.

ISBN 978-0-545-17855-6

10 9 8 7 6 5 4 3 2 1 10 11 12 13 14/0

Printed in the U.S.A. 40 • First printing, October 2010

SCHOLASTIC READER
LEVEL 1
50-250 WORDS

There's a Mouse in the House!

by Wendy Cheyette Lewison
illustrated by Hans Wilhelm

Cartwheel BOOKS®

SCHOLASTIC INC.
New York Toronto London Auckland
Sydney Mexico City New Delhi Hong Kong

Once there was a mouse
who walked into a house.

“Eek!” yelled the mommy.
“There’s a mouse in the house!”

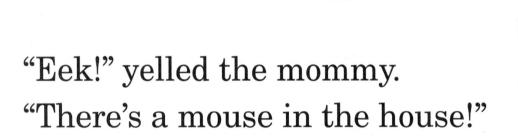

The mommy
said, “Go!”
But the mouse
said, “No.”

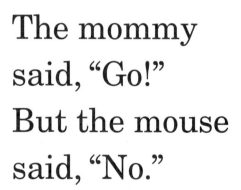

So the mommy
yelled again . . .

. . . and the daddy came in.
"Eek!" yelled the daddy.
"There's a mouse in the house!"

The daddy
said, "Go!"
But the mouse
said, "No."

So the daddy yelled again . . .

. . . and the grandma came in.

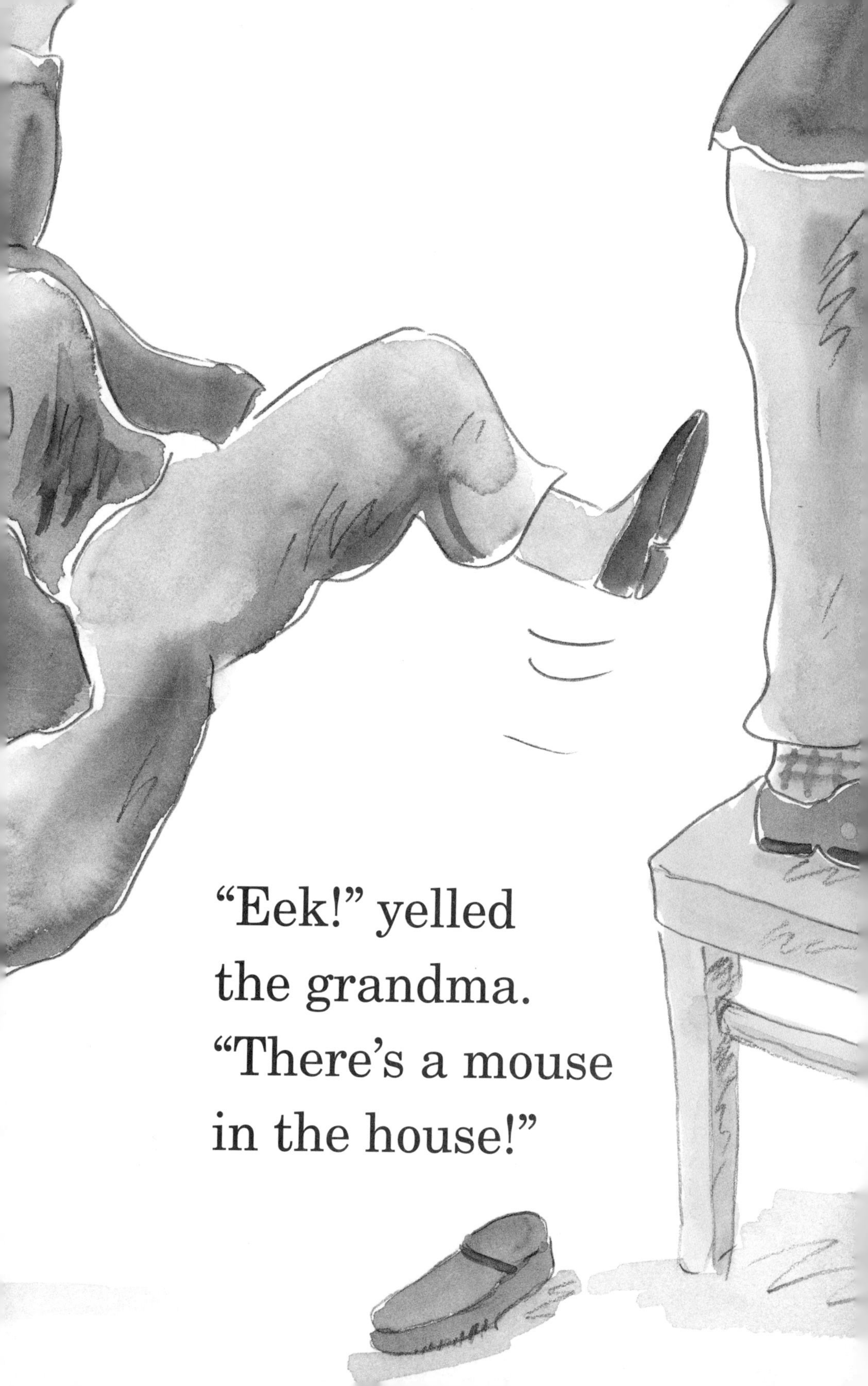

“Eek!” yelled
the grandma.
“There’s a mouse
in the house!”

The grandma said, “Go!”
But the mouse said, “No.”

So the grandma
yelled again . . .

. . . and the children came in.

“Ooh!” yelled the children.
“There’s a mouse in the house!”

And the children said, "Stay!"

Then the grandma said, "Stay?"

And the daddy said, “Stay?”

And the mommy said, “Stay?”

"Why, yes! You may!"

Then the mouse
said, "Okay!"

And he's still there today.